Clara Vulliamy

THE LOST PUPPY

Dotty DETECTIVE

HarperCollins *Children's Books*

First published in Great Britain by
HarperCollins *Children's Books* in 2017
First published in the United States of America in
this edition by HarperCollins *Children's Books* 2018
HarperCollins *Children's Books* is a
division of HarperCollins*Publishers* Ltd,
HarperCollins Publishers
1 London Bridge Street
London SE1 9GF

The HarperCollins website address is:
www.harpercollins.co.uk

1

ISBN 978-0-00-828245-5

Printed and bound by
CPI Group (UK) Ltd, Croydon, CR0 4YY

MIX
Paper from
responsible sources
FSC
www.fsc.org
FSC™ C007454

For my dear friend Kate Jessop,
with love

Read the whole series:

★ *Dotty Detective*

★ *Dotty Detective: The Pawprint Puzzle*

★ *Dotty Detective: The Midnight Mystery*

★ *Dotty Detective: The Lost Puppy*

Coming soon:

★ *Dotty Detective: The Birthday Surprise*

★ *Dotty Detective: The Vacation Mystery*

**This book
belongs to . . .**

DOT

and McClusky

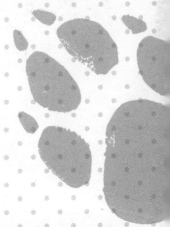

SUNDAY

This is me—Dot!

7

And this is TOP DOG, McClusky.

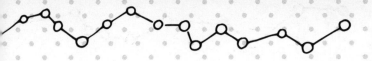

There is something *extremely important* you need to know...

Me and McClusky and our best pal Beans (who is in my class at school) are SUPER-SECRET AGENTS with our very own detective agency—the JOIN THE DOTS DETECTIVES! There is no mystery we cannot solve, however dastardly difficult.

But there is **NO TIME** to tell you more about that now!

JOIN THE DOTS DETECTIVES

I **JUMP** up out of bed and eat my favorite breakfast cereal (which is Honey Nut Crunchers) at *supersonic* speed

CRUNCH

SLURP.

I am having kittens with nerves ...

…because today I am trying out for the **HIGHFIELD HARRIERS**, our local running team!

Setting off for the park now—me, Mom, McClusky, and the twins (my brother and sister, Alf and Maisy).

Grandpa George is waiting for us at the park entrance. He takes the twins over to the swings so Mom can concentrate on cheering for me.

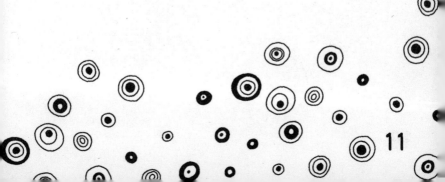

I'm actually a pretty *fast* runner.

Me and Mom do running training together every weekend.

I try my *absolute* hardest...

PHEW. It goes OK!

Really hope I get in.

McClusky has a busy morning in the park, too, meeting up with his friend, a big silly dog called Geoffrey. McClusky has a SERIOUSLY HECTIC social life.

Geoffrey belongs to Amy, who is also in my class at school.

He is HUGE—nearly as tall as her!

McClusky and Geoffrey
go **crazy** with joy
to see each other, chasing around
and around and around like lunatics

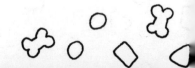

and playing **hide-and-seek** in the bushes.

McClusky spends all afternoon asleep in his bed, **EXHAUSTED.** But at dinnertime, just one rustle of the WaggyTail dog food bag and he's awake and up like a rocket.

Back in my room, which is also Join the Dots Detectives HQ— TOP SECRET! I'm packing my bag and getting ready for school tomorrow.

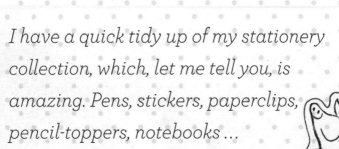

I have a quick tidy up of my stationery collection, which, let me tell you, is amazing. Pens, stickers, paperclips, pencil-toppers, notebooks … and polka dots on EVERYTHING!!

Looking forward to trying out my new super-sticky glow-in-the-dark spotted tape sometime soon.

This is going to be a GOOD week— it's nearly the end of school and that means it's nearly summer vacation! AND next Saturday it's the school summer fair!!!

Monday

Arriving at school, and there's a
FANTASTIC surprise waiting for us...

Joe Buckley has brought in his new
sausage dog puppy, Chorizo!

She is SOOOO CUTE!!!

It is her *first ever* outing. Puppies have to stay at home indoors for the first few weeks, but Joe has been telling us ALL about her.

Joe is not the only one who is excited…

McClusky and Geoffrey are over the moon to make a new friend!

The three dogs are tied to the railings because they aren't allowed in the playground.

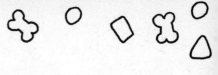

Chorizo is VERY wiggly and full of bounce.

She gets all tangled up with McClusky who starts barking and that sets off Geoffrey too.

What a **crazy** bunch the school gate gang are!

WOOF!

WOOF!

WOOF!

23

Lining up to go into the classroom, Joe tells us about some *funny* things Chorizo has done while she's been settling in to her new home.

"The other day, she hid in a cardboard tube and got **stuck**. She loves getting in the laundry basket, too. One time she burrowed right inside my mom's sweater and got trapped in the sleeve!"

Joe longed for a puppy for ages and ages but his family had to save up— sausage dogs are VERY expensive. What a difference to McClusky—he came from an animal rescue center!

Certificate of Adoption

This certifies that ....Dot...........
has officially adopted ....McClusky.......

I promise to give my dog
a forever home
of love, care and fun.
I will be his best friend always.

In class, we are all
super-excited
because of the **summer fair**.

Our teacher, Mr. Dickens, tells us
that our class will be in charge of
Pets Corner. He asks us all about
our pets. "Pets Corner will have a
guessing competition," he says.
"Guess the height of Geoffrey,
for instance … Any other ideas?"

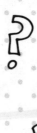

"Guess the length of Chorizo!" says Joe.

"You'll *never* guess my guinea pig's name!" Nadia calls out.

Roly-Poly?

Mr. Squeak?

?

Gordon?

Cheeky?

Caramel?

?

?

?

Bubbles?

"How about guess the **weight** of my S T I C K insect!" shouts Frankie Logan.

"I've got another one—how many biscuits in a

BIG

bag of dog food!" says Amy. "You won't *believe* how many Geoffrey gets through."

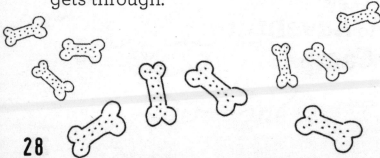

"Visitors to **Pets Corner** can pay for guesses, and the closest answers to each question will win a **PRIZE**," Mr. Dickens tells us.

I'm not sure what visitors could guess about McClusky. He's not extra TALL or SHORT or long. I'll think it over.

Beans says "I WISH I had a pet!" He still misses Norman, the earwig he met on the school trip to **Adventure Camp**.

"I'm going to design the world's **BEST** robot pet," he says.

Beans is **amazing** at inventing things.

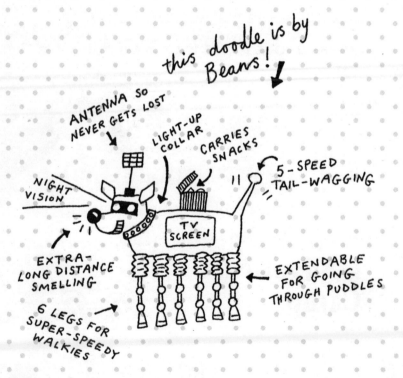

this doodle is by Beans!

ANTENNA SO NEVER GETS LOST

LIGHT-UP COLLAR

CARRIES SNACKS

5-SPEED TAIL-WAGGING

NIGHT VISION

TV SCREEN

EXTRA-LONG DISTANCE SMELLING

EXTENDABLE FOR GOING THROUGH PUDDLES

6 LEGS FOR SUPER-SPEEDY WALKIES

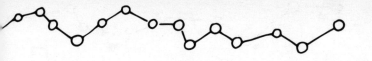

We are all chatting about what we will do at the fair.

"There's going to be a **popcorn** machine!" says Fiyaz.

"AND a **bounce** house!" adds Kirstie.

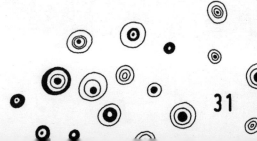

"I'll be playing my trumpet in the brass band performance," says Marcus. Then we all **loudly** pretend to be playing in the brass band too … until Frankie is *too* **wild** with his imaginary trombone and knocks over his chair.

TOOT!
TOOT!

"OK, you noisy crew," says Mr. D., "we need to get to work now."

We don't mind though because this work will be *fun*...

Mr. D. tells us that this week, to get in the mood for the fair, we will learn about **South American carnivals!**

TUEsdAy

At the school gates Chorizo is even more *wiggly*. She keeps getting in everybody's way and tripping people up.

Kirstie's dad laughs and says, "She shouldn't be left lying around—someone might **STEAL** her!"

"AWWW she's so lovely," says Milo's mom. "She would make such a cozy hot-water bottle!"

At lunchtime, Mrs. Bagshott, our principal, asks for helpers to put up bunting all around the playground.

Me, Beans, and Amy have a *really*

looooong...

piece of bunting, blue and yellow,
which are the school colors. We tie
it up on to the railings, as high as we
can reach.

It's a bit higher at one end and lower at the other, because Amy is tallest, then Beans, then me.

But it all looks really good.

Getting **SO IMPATIENT** for the day of the fair to arrive!

In Music, Mr. D. shows us a film in the hall about Samba drumming from Brazil. It is **SO cool**.

We have a try ourselves, with drums and also tambourines, bells, and whistles. **VERY noisy!**

Mr. Meades comes
in to sweep ...
and does a little
dance with his
broom.

As we are packing
our bags to go home,
Mr. Dickens says, "You'll NEVER
GUESS what I will be doing at the
fair! It's going to be a

BIG surprise ... "

He is *always* teasing us!

 After supper, I am relaxing in my room and thinking about summer vacation.

 Me and my family are not actually going away anywhere but we will be having lots of *awesome* DAY TRIPS.

Beans is staying at home too, so Mom says he can join in with some of our outings if he likes. Top of our list is the outdoor swimming pool, a picnic at Westbury Farm Park ...

AND Beans's Auntie Celia says she will take us **GO-KARTING!**

WOOO
Hoooo!!!

We are in a

to get to school today. First, Maisy
forgets the dragon drawing she
wanted to bring to Nursery School
so we have to go back for it ...

And then Alf suddenly remembers
a very important pebble he wanted
to bring, so we have to go back
AGAIN...

And *at last* I arrive at school.

During attendance we are **all** trying to guess what Mr. D.'s surprise is.

"Ju_ggling?"

"NO."

"Doing a *dance* with Mrs. Bagshott?"

"NO."

"Giving everybody **FREE** ice cream?"

"NO."

We have **NO IDEA** what it could be.

In Science, me, Beans, Fiyaz, and Nadia are in a group for our South American-rainforest-animals project.

We head over to the computer lab to research the most **unusual** animals we can find—caimans, anteaters, civets ...

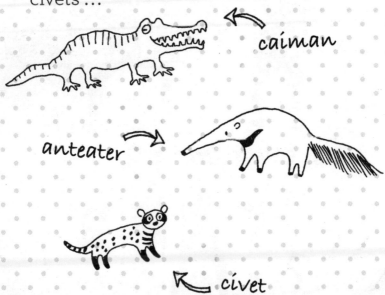

caiman

anteater

civet

We choose a capybara to focus on, which is a *bit* like a guinea pig but

HUGE.

HUGE! ↑

↑ PRETTY SMALL

Now THAT would be an exciting guest in **Pets Corner!!!**

It's absolute **CHAOS** in the playground at going-home time. The **bounce** house is being delivered by van. Food for the BBQ and the big bag of dog food for **Pets Corner**

STORE ROOM

is being carried into Mr. Meades's storeroom and the stage is being assembled.

In all the muddle of crowds and people *coming* and *going* it takes me ages to find Mom! But when we come out of the school gate to fetch McClusky...

Chorizo has **GONE.**

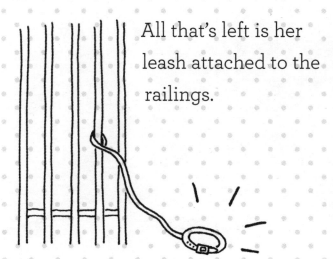

All that's left is her leash attached to the railings.

Joe is *really* upset, but his mom says, "Don't worry, Joe, we'll soon find her. She couldn't have gone very far on those little legs."

Everybody promises to keep their
EYES PEELED.

"Which way did she go, McClusky?"
I ask. But he isn't listening. He seems
more interested in Mr. Meades
carrying a **huge** box of burgers
across the playground.

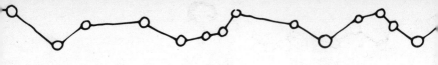

We can't help worrying about Chorizo
as we walk back from school. She is
too young to know her way home.
I ask Mom to text Joe's mom:

Any luck?

but the answer comes back:

Not yet.

We search every front yard and
every bush on the way home,
but there is **no sign** of Chorizo
anywhere.

On the corner of the street where I go one way and Beans goes the other, there is just time for a super-quick **JOIN THE DOTS DETECTIVES** meeting.

Join the Dots Detectives HQ

"This is a *REAL* mystery," I whisper, "and we have the *perfect* detective skills to find Chorizo!"

"YES!" whispers Beans. "We have already solved lots of cases AND we've got McClusky to help us!"

We decide that the first thing to do is look for clues and find witnesses. Somebody *must* have seen her.

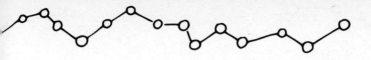

Wherever she is, we will find her.
The **JOIN THE DOTS DETECTIVES**
are **ON THE CASE!**

Back at Dot HQ, I get to work making a LOST poster. This calls for my very best pens from my stationery collection.

LOST!
SAUSAGE DOG
PUPPY CALLED
CHORIZO

It needs to go across three pieces of paper, because Chorizo is so long: one for her tail end, one for her middle section, and one for her nose end.

IF YOU SEE HER
PLEASE BRING HER
BACK TO *JOE*
AT OAKFIELD SCHOOL

After dinner, Mom is

experimenting

in the kitchen.

She is trying out a **new** recipe for cupcakes, which she will be baking for the fair.

There are bowls of different icing on the table—**peanut butter**, mint chocolate chip, *Turkish delight*, **strawberries and cream** ...

Me and the twins help by each bringing a spoon and trying them. It takes *quite a few spoonfuls* for us to give our final definite opinions on which we like **best**.

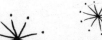

I have a

bright

idea!

I ask Mom for a cupcake as a special treat in my lunchbox, but *really* it is to send a secret message to Beans.

I borrow a glitter-writing icing tube, and write a secret message on the cake.

Thursday

On the way to school, I put up the LOST poster. It sticks up really well with my *glow-in-the-dark spotted tape!*

We search in bushes and yards again, calling out Chorizo's name.

CHORIZO!

CHORIZO!

CHORIZO!

In class, Joe is sad. Chorizo hasn't turned up yet.

We try to cheer him up. "Don't worry, she'll be home again really soon, you'll see!"

At recess, I give Beans the cake.

MEET ME AT THE LOOKOUT!

Super-speedily, we split the cupcake into two and eat it, so no one else can read it.

We are in **the Lookout**, which is our secret meeting place in the playground.

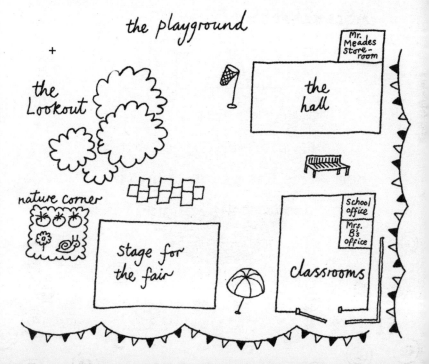

the playground

the Lookout

nature corner

the hall

Mr. Meades store-room

stage for the fair

classrooms

School office

Mrs. B's office

Beans says, "You *could* have just told me that we needed to meet here—why the cupcake?"

But I say, "It's **good** to keep practicing our detective skills— and it's a lot more *fun* to write a SECRET MESSAGE you can EAT!"

"It's a lot more tasty, too," agrees Beans. He has a blob of mint chocolate chip icing on his nose.

"Now let's make a map of the area, so we can do a thorough search," I say. Beans is

A GENIUS

at maps.

We figure out that as Chorizo can only walk a little way on her short legs, she couldn't have gotten far.

We draw a circle to show the search area.

Inside the circle we put a **★star★** next to the *special* places of interest we think she could be.

"What about a list of possible witnesses?" I ask. "People to speak to who might have seen something ..."

Moms and dads

Paws Awhile owner

Butcher

Pink Vanilla Café owner

Park keeper

Ice-cream truck driver

We are very pleased with our map—
it's a good place to start.

For Spelling today we play "silent
letters snakes and ladders".

We roll a dice and move along the
snakes and ladders board. Every
time we land on a square there is a
spelling question with a silent letter
in it to answer, like the "K" in "knot".

Get it right,
you go up
the ladder.

Get it wrong—*down the snake!*

It's **SO TRICKY!**

I get a ladder because I got "gnome" right (HOORAY!) but a snake with ~~rubarb~~ "rhubarb".

Amy who sits at my table is first to get all of hers right. Beans is struggling with "gnu," and Frankie Logan isn't really trying at all ...

He is doing an impression of a gnat
and sends a pencil pot flying.

"Calamity custard!" says Mr. D.
"There's never anything silent about
you, Frankie!"

At lunchtime, me and Beans sit with
Joe. We show him the map of the
search area, places of interest, and
possible witnesses. He thinks it's
really great. We all share my mango
slices.

In Science, me and my Rainforest group are finding FACTS about camouflage. It's AMAZING how smart some animals are.

Here is a chameleon *pretending* to be a leaf!

At going-home time, Joe shows the map to his mom. She says, "Thank you so much, this is REALLY HELPFUL."

"We want to search with you!" I say. "Can we, Mom?"

Mom says we should all help to search. Beans and his dad are eager. Lots of other parents at the school gates overhear and agree to help too.

Mr. D. asks, "What can I do?" And I say, "We need leaflets to hand out!" He borrows a photograph from Joe's

Mom, and our map; and rushes back into the school office. A few minutes later, he returns with lots of leaflets.

MISSING!

Have YOU seen Chorizo?

Last seen at Oakfield School
PLEASE CALL!

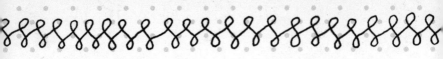

We split up into groups to search.
Our group is me, Beans, Frankie, our
parents, and the twins and McClusky,
too, of course.

Heading up to the main street first.
We stop at each shop, asking if
anyone has seen Chorizo.

Everybody we speak to is very kind
and sympathetic, but **no one** has
seen her.

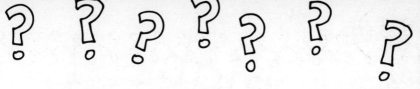

We leave a leaflet at each place, to go in the window.

Now we are in the park. Luckily it's a summer evening and still light, which gives us more time.

I think back to Sunday when McClusky was playing with Geoffrey, trying to remember all the places that dogs especially like.

We search  high and l o w

although
since she has
such little
legs there's
not much
point in high.

"I don't think
she could
be up a tree,
Frankie!!!"
I say.

Even the twins are doing their part, looking in the tall grass and flowerbeds.

Could she be camouflaged somehow? I look closely at **muddy** places and soil which are dark brown like Chorizo.

Then Beans remembers something. "Joe told us she got stuck in a **cardboard tube**—and the sleeve of a sweater! Look out for **long**, thin things, everybody!"

There's the gardener's hose, but that's too small. The tunnel to crawl through in the playground, but that's too big.

No sign of Chorizo **anywhere.**

And there is something **very strange** about McClusky. He doesn't show any interest in looking. He pulls on his leash to go back the way we came, *whining*.

He is being lazy and wants to go home! I am completely mystified—doesn't he CARE?

Mom texts Joe's mom and the other search parties. They decide to call it a day and try again tomorrow, so we all head home.

Dinner is huge bowls of spaghetti with meat sauce. We are all SO hungry.

At bedtime, I look in my **FRED FANTASTIC'S CRAZY CRIME CAPERS** book for inspiration.

Fred Fantastic is an **ACE** detective on TV. With his cool sidekick Flo,

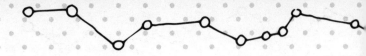

there is no case, however fiendishly tricky, they cannot solve. They search the mean streets of the big city for clues, and never give up until they find the evidence they need.

The **JOIN THE DOTS DETECTIVES** think that **FRED FANTASTIC'S** Five Golden Rules for solving a mystery are *ALWAYS* really useful …

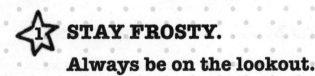 **STAY FROSTY.**
Always be on the lookout.

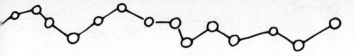

 FOLLOW THAT HUNCH!
If you've got a funny feeling,
you may be on to something
important.

 USE YOUR NOODLE.
Think!

 LOOK FOR A LIGHT-BULB
MOMENT.
A sudden genius idea.

 GET PROOF.
You MUST have the evidence
before you can solve your case.

I read a story about how Fred
travelled all the way

ACROSS

AMERICA

on a Greyhound bus (which doesn't
have a greyhound driving it, it just
means it is very fast) in search
of the final piece of evidence in
his case, only to find it was in his
pocket all along.

I don't think this helps us much.

"USE YOUR NOODLE, *DOT!*" I say to myself.

What can we try next???

Friday

"COME ON—WE ARE GOING TO BE

LATE

FOR SCHOOL!"

Mom is saying.

But we are all waiting by the front door while she searches for her keys.

I am

rushing  through the
school gate. McClusky tries to follow,
LONGING to rush through the gate
with me. It takes ALL Mom's strength
to hold him back.

"Is it because you *really miss me*
during the day, McClusky?" I ask him.

In the classroom, we are all talking
about where we have been looking
for Chorizo.

"I waited outside the butcher's for HOURS," says Marcus.

"The *butcher's,* Marcus??" we ask.

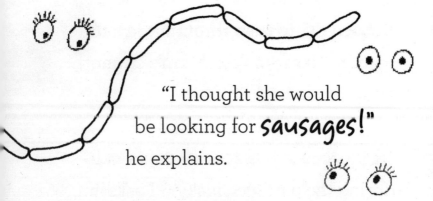

"I thought she would be looking for **sausages!**" he explains.

Laura (who is definitely NOT my friend usually) says she and her mom have been out looking too. I am really glad she is joining in.

But still no sightings, no clues.

"Don't worry, Joe," we say, "she will turn up again really soon!"

But secretly we are thinking that she must be getting farther and farther away by now.

"If Chorizo was lost, someone would have seen her by now, surely?" Beans says to me quietly when Joe has walked away.

An **awful** thought starts to grow in my head.

What if she is not hiding but someone is *deliberately*

hiding

her???

No time to talk about it now though— Mr. D. tells us to go to our places for quiet reading. I will have to wait until recess.

However down in the dumps
we are feeling, the **fair** must go on.

In Art we are making decorations for
Pets Corner out of colored paper
and collage.

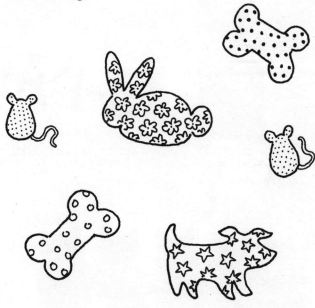

I fold a long piece of black paper into an accordion and cut out a cat shape.

When I open it up—

ta-DA!

—it's a garland of cats!

In PE, Mr. D. shows us how to dance the Bossa Nova.

I am always in a dance pair with Frankie. Although he is often crashing around in the classroom causing chaos, it turns out that he has *hidden talents*...

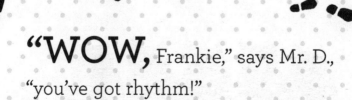

"**WOW,** Frankie," says Mr. D., "you've got rhythm!"

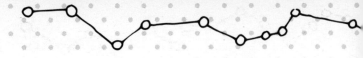

At recess, I RUSH to the Lookout with Beans …

"Do you remember at the school gates, when Chorizo was really wiggly and kept tripping people up?" I ask Beans. "What was it that Kirstie's dad said??

"Someone might steal her!"

"OH NO—that's **TERRIBLE!**" says Beans. "She must be very valuable. Joe said she cost a lot of money …"

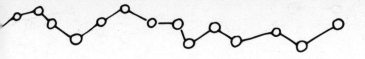

The more we think about it, the more convinced we are. What other explanation could there be? The case has now taken a disastrous, **VILLAINOUS** turn!

Chorizo
has been

STOLEN!!!!!

"We must write a list of suspects," I say.

Kirstie's dad?
Milo's mom?
the bounce house van driver?
the BBQ delivery person?
someone just passing by?

Kirstie's dad?

He is at the top of the list!

Milo's mom?

"She would make a such a cozy hot-water bottle!" we heard her say.

Maybe *she* stole Chorizo?

But it could be someone we don't even know ... the bounce-house-van driver? The BBQ delivery person? Someone just passing by?

The worst thing is, it could be

anybody ...

How **could** McClusky let Chorizo get stolen—Geoffrey yes, he's not too bright, but McClusky??

Heading back into class after recess, still *whispering* about our suspects and what our next move should be.

We are walking behind Mrs. Bagshott and we overhear her saying, "I've got a new one, a **beautiful dark brown—so soft** and SO sweet!"

We look at each other. Eyes **wide** with shock.

Could Mrs. Bagshott be talking about Chorizo????

"We need to get as close to Mrs. Bagshott as we can—find out more!" I say urgently to Beans.

Beans looks extremely nervous, but he nods his head: **YES.**

"FOLLOW THAT HUNCH, Dot!"
Beans says.

"STAY FROSTY, Beans!" I say.

In Art, we are finishing the decorations
for Pets Corner. But we can hardly
concentrate. I have accidentally drawn

THREE
EYES

on one of my paper cats without
thinking!

"We must get closer to Mrs. Bagshott's office!" I whisper to Beans.

It is SO SCARY

to spy on the principal (and she is quite scary anyway!!) but *the stakes are high*. We MUST save Chorizo, and do the right thing for Joe!

At lunchtime, we creep along the corridor and hide behind her office door …

"I'm terrified!" Beans whispers.
"What if she finds us spying on her?
We are going to be in **BIG**
TROUBLE!"

At first we can't hear anything clearly,
just muffled voices and the opening
and shutting of a cupboard drawer.
But *then* ...

"It's **so warm** and silky and SO
LONG!" Mrs. Bagshott is saying.
"Someone just left it outside the
school. No one seems to want it.
I think I'll take it home and keep it!"

So it's **TRUE!**

MRS. BAGSHOTT

STOLE

CHORIZO!!!!

We are completely *horrified.*

We hurry back to the classroom
before anyone sees us.

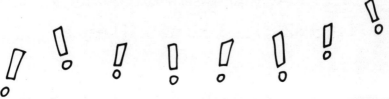

In Math I am doing an extra-tricky worksheet on circumferences and diameters, which usually I LOVE, but today I just stare at the page, not even seeing.

At going-home time, I whisper to Beans, "This is our last chance to get Chorizo back! *Come on,* QUICK!"

We come out of the main door with everybody else, but then slip around the corner and duck down behind a low wall.

We creep along to just outside
Mrs. Bagshott's office. My heart
is

THUMPING

in my chest.
But there's no turning back now!

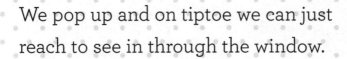

We pop up and on tiptoe we can just
reach to see in through the window.

And there she is, putting on her coat,
picking up her bag, and stroking ...
a long **soft** brown ...

SCARF,

with tiny rabbits
embroidered on it.

Our hearts sink into our boots,
hopes of finding Chorizo dashed.

"I was SO SURE we had the culprit," says Beans, as we walk home.

"We were **barking** up the wrong tree," I say.

This doesn't mean we were *actually* barking up a real tree …

WOOF! WOOF!

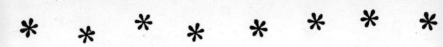

It means we followed the wrong lead and made a mistake.

I feel *terrible* about it. We were so sure we have the *perfect* detective skills to find Chorizo, but so far—

NOTHING.

With every day that goes by I worry more and more about her.

For dinner, Mom makes us peas and rice which is usually my favorite, but I hardly touch it. She has saved three

spare cupcakes especially for us but
I don't even
want one.

It's evening and I'm just fetching a
drink of water in the kitchen.

McClusky is **whining** and *whimpering*.
Is he trying to tell me something?

He pulls his bag of WaggyTail dog
food over to me and looks expectant.
His tail is *whirring* like a propeller.

"How *could* you think about **dinner** at a time like this, McClusky?!?"

I just don't know what to do.

Poor puppy. And poor Joe!

Saturday

All morning I'm worrying about the fair. **Pets Corner** just won't be the same with Chorizo **missing**. We will be feeling sad about her the whole time. I'm sure Joe won't even want to be there.

McClusky does, though—he's been ready and waiting at the front door **since breakfast!**

I try some **tricky** word searches in my puzzle book to relax, but I just can't concentrate.

Mom gives us each a little bit of spending money for the fair. I pop it safely in my change purse.

I have a change purse shaped like an ice-cream cone. Alf has a piglet change purse and Maisy has a change purse in the shape of a Tyrannosaurus Rex.

We arrive at school early to get **Pets Corner** ready.

Me, Beans, and Nadia help Mr. D. to put up the enclosure and decorate it.

Mr. Meades is busy *rushing to and fro,* bringing the BBQ food from his storeroom and helping to inflate the **bounce** house.

The school choir, recorder group and brass band are all practicing different songs at the same time which makes a terrible noise!

Parents are setting up **exciting-looking** stalls, and there's a

delicious smell

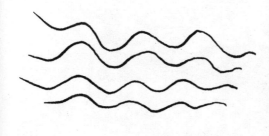

wafting over from the **p**o**pcorn** machine.

As soon as McClusky is put inside the **Pets Corner** enclosure, he tries desperately to JUMP out. It must be his delight at actually being inside the playground at last. Maybe he wants to explore?

I am embarrassed by McClusky's over-excitement in front of Joe. "We didn't think you would come," we say to Joe.

"Would you like to hold my stick insect?" asks Frankie kindly.

McClusky is looking at me **SO intensely**.

"What *is* it, McClusky?" I ask him.

He has been acting so strangely lately! It just doesn't make sense …

I think back to when he was *pulling* on his leash during the search and I thought he was being lazy and wanting to go home ... but perhaps it wasn't *home* he was trying to drag us back to ...

I remember when he tried to **rush** in though the school gate with me ...

And then last night he was *desperately* trying to show me his bag of dog food ...

It all clicks into place ...

I have a **LIGHT-BULB MOMENT!**

"McClusky KNOWS where Chorizo is!"

I say to Beans. "He has known right from the very start. He's been trying to tell us *all along* in his own doggy way, and we didn't realize!"

We let McClusky go and he takes off at great speed across the playground, barking loudly.

I RUN after him, and Beans runs

after me. (Lucky I've picked up some speed in my training with Mom!)

McClusky leads us straight to Mr. Meades's storeroom. He keeps on barking and barking outside the door…

And then we hear another dog **barking** back.

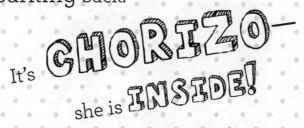

It's CHORIZO— she is INSIDE!

Will she be **hungry**, *frightened*, **cold**, and m i s e r a b l e??

NO!

Chorizo is *extremely fine* and **happy**, snuggled up warmly under Mr. Meades's old wool sweater!

She must have been so cozily **fast asleep** she hadn't even noticed when Mr. Meades came in and out fetching things for the fair. It was only McClusky's

VERY
LOUD

barking that finally woke her up.

She has been feasting on the **big** bag of dog food for the "*Guess How Many Biscuits*" competition, and drinking from a tub of water Mr. Meades keeps for watering his geraniums.

She must have followed the food, slipped in unnoticed when the door was ajar and got shut in.

Mr. Meades has been too busy and distracted to notice her.

Chorizo wasn't **LOST OR STOLEN** ...

She was right under our noses all along!

McClusky and Chorizo are **SO HAPPY** to see each other. There is LOTS of tail-wagging.

We take Chorizo over to Joe who is absolutely **on top of the world**.

Joe's mom rushes over. She is all smiles and everybody **hugs** everybody else.

Pets Corner is a

GREAT

SUCCESS—

who knew

that a stick insect weighs so little,

or that Nadia's guinea pig is called

waffles?

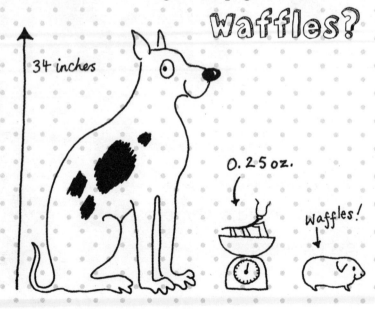

34 inches

0.25 oz.

Waffles!

Guessing the number of biscuits isn't going to be **too challenging** as its clear to see there are only a few left in the dog-food bag.

"Lucky for Chorizo it's her length and not the circumference of her belly that is being guessed!" we whisper to each other SECRETLY.

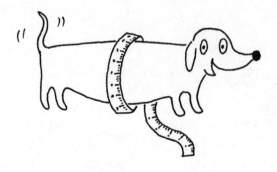

I wasn't sure what visitors to **Pets Corner** could guess about McClusky, but I do know now. It is to guess his extra-special genius skill.

He is SO SMART

and has a great nose for sniffing out the clues—the **ACE DETECTIVE** who found the lost puppy!

You can measure a tall dog and weigh a stick insect and count the dog biscuits, but you just cannot measure how much of a star McClusky has been in the **JOIN THE DOTS DETECTIVES**. He was giving us messages that were the *vital clues* all along.

"I am SO SO SORRY, McClusky," I say to him. "How could I ever have doubted you?"

He gives me a lick as if to say, "That's OK! We are a GREAT team!"

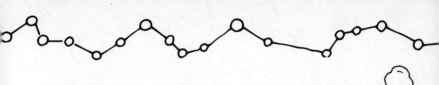

Me, Beans, and Joe go around the **fair** visiting all the stalls.

Joe's mom buys us each an

extra-big bag

of fresh **p⁰pcorn**,

and a NEW
squeaky toy
for McClusky.

squeak!

I win a small panda bear
key-ring at the Teddy Raffle,
and Beans has his face painted
as an **ALIEN**.

We have lots of tries at the **PRICKLY
PORCUPINE** game…

You pick out one of prickles (which
are really made from cocktail sticks)
and the ones with a colored end

get a **prize**. Joe wins some **fruit candy** and shares it with us.

The twins are having a great time
too. They spend **ages** on the
bounce house, and Mom buys
them each a daisy at the plant stall.

Grandpa George makes
several visits to the afternoon-tea
stall for *strawberry cream scones.*

We watch the **karate display**,
the **choir**, the **brass band**,
the **recorders** …

And now there are loud whoops and
cheers and here comes Mr. Dickens …

He is a

ONE-MAN BAND!!!

He plays a squeezebox and a harmonica
and cymbals and a **HUGE**

drum *all at the same time*, and sings
some **VERY** funny songs.

So *that* was his surprise!

"What a day!" says Mom, as we sit on the sofa together before bedtime. The phone rings …

Some good news! I HAVE got into the **HIGHFIELD HARRIERS!**

YESSS!!!

I am on CLOUD NINE …

Another case solved.

What will the next fiendishly tricky mystery be?

Have you read?

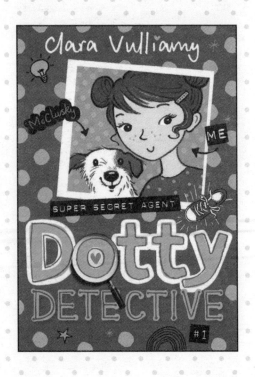

When someone seems set on sabotaging the school show, Dot is determined to find out how, and save the day!

When Dot starts hearing strange noises
at night, Beans is convinced there has to
be something SPOOKY afoot. But, before
they can be certain, Dot and Beans must
GET PROOF.

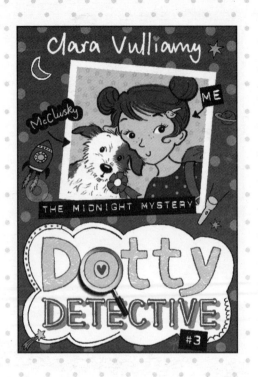

Dot and Beans can't wait for their school
trip to Adventure Camp where they will do
lots of exciting adventure activities and
may even win the Adventurers' Prize!
But why is someone trying to spoil the fun?

Join Dot, Beans, and McClusky
on their next case…

LOOK OUT FOR ANOTHER

Dotty
DETECTIVE

coming soon…